# Under the Eye Of the Magpie

## by ALICE E. SMITH

*Illustrated by Sandra Hecht*
*Cover by Harold Eckert*
*Edited by LaVonne Nerge*

PRESS

*Under the Eye of the Magpie*
by Alice E. Smith

Printed in the United States of America

ISBN 9781609573065

www.xulonpress.com

# Table of Contents

# INTRODUCTION

W hen I was very young, I played in the sand
pile and dug deep holes. Like many children, I pretended I was digging to China. While
growing up on a farm in southern Minnesota in the
United States of America, I never dreamed that I
would someday actually visit China and live in Asia
for thirteen years. How did that happen?

My husband and I were teachers. Schools in Asia
needed teachers with our skills, so in 1979, we moved
to Hong Kong with our two young sons. For three
years we worked at the Hong Kong International
School and lived in Stanley, a fishing village on the
southern tip of Victoria Island. At that time Hong
Kong was still a British Colony. In another book, I

will share some of the interesting things we saw and experienced while we lived there.

After returning to the USA so that my husband could complete seminary training, we were assigned to Hillcrest School in Jos, Nigeria, West Africa. Students at that school came from all over West Africa where their parents were serving as Christian missionaries. God willing, several chapters will fill another book to tell about the interesting things we experienced during our two years in Africa.

While our sons were in high school and college, we lived in the USA. After our sons married, we accepted teaching positions at Seoul Foreign School and worked there for five years. This book, UNDER THE EYE OF THE MAGPIE, was inspired by people and places we saw while living in South Korea.

Our final five years in Asia were spent in Indonesia. In the future, I hope to write more about our life and work in this wonderful tropical country.

I hope you will enjoy reading my book. If you care to email me, my address is: alicesaddress@ yahoo.com

# Acknowledgments

This book has been in my dreams for many years. To have it become a reality is to have my dreams come true. The inspiration for the book came during an actual trip to Cheju-do in the year 2000. Our friends, Jeremy and Liz were members of the faculty with us at Seoul Foreign School. Liz and I had recently completed our Master's Degree in Education. Our husbands wanted to do something special for us, so they arranged the trip for the four of us to fly to Cheju-do. As we were touring the island, I kept a journal of our experiences. The plot for the book formed in my mind at that time. I quickly jotted it down in my journal and then put it away for a few years.

During a trip to the island of Bali in 2003, I began to work on the written text but did not have time to finish it. Because I was working full time, I decided I would not work on it again until after my retirement. The perfect time came at the beginning of 2010, when I was finally able to spend long stretches of quiet time to work at my computer.

I am grateful to my dear husband, Bob, for encouraging me along the way. He has been a great cheer-leader and constructive critic. I owe many thanks to my illustrators, Sandy Hecht and Harold Eckert, whose sketches capture my visions so well. My personal editor, LaVonne Nerge is a jewel of great worth. Her careful reading polished my rough drafts.

I am grateful to all the students and teachers at Seoul Foreign School. This strong Christian community is a rare mixture of professionalism, respect, high expectations, and rewarding achievement. Lifetime skills developed at SFS by teachers and students are deep, rich, and enduring. Friendships built here last a lifetime. To have been a part of all it brings tears to my eyes!

Finally, I wish to end these acknowledgements in the manner following Johann Sebastian Bach, who ended his compositions with the initials S.D.G. I would like to do the same. In Latin, these letters stand for Soli Deo Gloria, meaning, "TO GOD ALONE BE THE GLORY!"

~ To my beloved grandchildren ~

Sophia Evangeline
Jeffrey Michael
Naomi Irene
Timothy Ryan
Ellesha Loreen
Scott Thomas William
Kennedy Albert
Christina Marie

*Real heroes may not always be adults.*
*Age has nothing to do with it.*
*You can make a difference no matter*
*what age you are.*

*Austin Gutwein*

# 1.

# A Bird's Eye View

Yazdee, the gossipy magpie, had seen it all. She had been sitting on her brood of eggs in a messy nest of twigs and trash now for more than a week. One egg was noticeably larger than the others. It had been secretly deposited by a flighty neighborhood cuckoo bird. Yazdee allowed for it to remain, following an instinctive habit that existed between the feathered species.

Perched high in the trees bordering Seoul Foreign School and overlooking Yonhi Manor, days passed quickly as Yazdee followed every movement and watched the mystery unfold. Her eyes were sharp and her recollection was keen. She had not missed a thing. If birds could talk, she would have explained everything.

"Keep your arms out for balance! You can do it!" Emily yelled at Annie. The plump ten-year-old sucked in her breath and bit her bottom lip as she felt her wobbly legs lock into place. She was doing it! She was up and coasting along the sidewalk on her new roller blades!

"Now I'm moving, but how do I...I...I... STOP!?" Annie hit the sidewalk with a loud smack! ....."OUCH!"

"Not like that!" quipped Emily. "Are you okay?"

"Ouch, it hurts!" cried Annie. "My knee is bleeding!"

"Come on, I'll help you up."

It was a week-end at Seoul Foreign School. A radiant abundance of azaleas, tulips, and daffodils fulfilled the promise of spring. The E building picnic area was alive with toddlers learning how to walk. Close behind, *amahs*, the family maids, followed to cushion their awkward falls. On the sidewalks, brave young children attempted to balance on their two-wheelers. Beyond the wall, joggers streaked along the tree-lined trails of Yonsi University.

Most of the teachers and their families lived here, with easy access to the classrooms. A sturdy high wall and a uniformed security team guarded the campus around the clock. Located in Yonhi Dong, the school had a long and respectable history. In 1912 it began as a school in Seoul for the children of Christian missionaries. As the years passed, it evolved into an international school, while maintaining a Christian worldview. Well-trained and highly qualified Christian teachers from around the globe worked here. Composed of students with foreign passports only, the annual enrollment hung steadily around 1200 pupils.

Mr. Van was a sixth grade teacher. His wife Lilly also taught at SFS, and their children attended the school. Their fifth floor apartment in the F building overlooked the entire campus. The school soccer field was visible from their wide living room windows.

Yazdee kept a sharp eye on Tigger, their family cat. She intended to keep her nestlings far from this tricky predator. This sly cat was a skilled hunter. The campus was the center of his broad kingdom. He confidently roamed every inch of it. More than once, the magpie had swooped the feline as he silently stalked an innocent victim.

Although Tigger did manage outside hunts, he actually preferred to lounge inside the apartment on his purple velvet cushion.

*Tigger's cushion*

His first choice was to dine on expensive gourmet Cat Cuisine the Vans purchased from the Saruga supermarket. Yazdee felt only disgust for this uppity and finicky big gray cat.

Most of the students at SFS were bused to school from various districts (*dongs*) of the city of Seoul. Nearly a dozen motor coaches were housed in a huge bus garage at the edge of the soccer field. A team of bus drivers proudly managed the mechanical upkeep and sleek appearance of the entire fleet. Today, a bus was parked under Yazdee's tree. The bus drivers had scrubbed it clean using mops and buckets of sudsy water. It was spotless!

***The bus was spotless!***

Five mornings a week, Yazdee listened with fascination as the heavy vehicles labored up the steep paved road. Reaching the top of the winding driveway, their brakes loudly squeaked to a stop. The bus doors popped open, and each vehicle spit out a load of noisy students. The whole scene rapidly reversed at the close of the day as the buses lined up, inhaled their passengers, and twisted down the hill.

A number of school families lived in Yonhi Manor, an apartment complex nestled into the hillside just below SFS. The Baptist Mission managed this property, which was bordered by sturdy walls of light brown brick. Many of the families were assisted by maids, nannies and drivers during their stay as business and professional workers in South Korea. A hired security team guarded the shiny brass gate at the main entrance.

Yazdee found pleasure in following the movements of the smartly uniformed security men. Their guard house was built like a tiny pagoda complete with a roof of red clay tiles. Large windows on three sides made for a perfect view by the curious bird. She watched as the guards registered the identification of all who entered or exited the compound.

The bird also noticed the guards were oblivious to the movements of any birds or animals, other than scattering a few food scraps or bread crumbs for them now and then. Of course, Tigger only sniffed at these inferior offerings. His trips through the gate were for hunting purposes only.

# 2.

# Making Plans

"**M**r. Van! Do you have our tickets yet?" shouted Annie as she bounced into the classroom.

"Not yet. The travel agent emailed me this morning. She needs a copy of everyone's passport before they will issue our group tickets." Mr. Van had once again organized this annual class trip as a culminating activity for the sixth-grade unit on Korean Culture.

Aware of the affluence of his students, Mr. Van believed a flight to Cheju-do could be financially managed by the sixth-graders. His hunch had proven correct. With school scholarships providing for those who needed assistance, this was the third year for the entire sixth grade to make the trip.

By Wednesday he had copies of passports. After faxing them to the travel agent, the bundle of tickets arrived on Thursday. Brian and Steve, two tall sixth-graders, were the first to spot the fat manila envelope in Mr. Van's hand. "We're off!" they shouted.

"Not so fast," responded Mr. Van. Stepping toward a bookshelf behind his desk, he reached for a file bin. He pulled out a handful of maps and several copies of blank books. "Please put one of these on every student's desk." Eager to please, the boys soon had all the desks supplied. The maps would be used to highlight the path of the trip, and the blank books would be used as journals to record their reflections while traveling.

As more students arrived, noisy clatter filled the room. Chairs hit the floor with a thud as they were downloaded from the desktops. The electric pencil sharpener buzzed again and again. Notebooks clicked as homework sheets were removed and placed into their respective trays. Popsicle sticks, printed with individual student's names, were removed from the attendance chart and placed in the container on Mr. Van's desk. Later in the day, he randomly removed sticks from the container and used the names to call on people for discussions. Chattering girls roamed back and forth from the doorway, watching for friends as they checked in for the day. The energetic boys and girls filled the room like a noisy flock of birds settling down unto a feeding area.

The school day was about to begin. Steve picked up his red and black pencil and leaned back in his chair. As he did so, a metal keychain dropped from his pocket and rattled to the floor. It was a treasure from his friend Mark. Mark was a year older and had gone on the Cheju-do trip last year when he was a sixth grader. Mark and Steve were always trading treasures. He had traded two cat-eyed marbles for this key chain. Not bad, he thought. Steve picked it up and turned it over in his hand. It was a replica of a *mape*.

Antique circular *mapes* in various sizes were sold all over Korea. They had an interesting history.

Hundreds of years ago, authentic *mapes* were given to messengers by their warlords. These polished metal medallions were inscribed with the king's official signature on one side. The opposite side was stamped with a certain number of images of horses. A *mape* with six horses indicated that the message was of extreme importance.

A lower number of horse images meant that the message was of less importance.

As Steve rubbed his thumb over the surface of the tiny *mape*, Claire poked him and whispered that she wanted to look at it. Steve quietly placed it on her desk. Claire hoped they would find some of these neat souvenirs on the island. She wanted to give *mapes* with six horses to Annie and Emily, her closest friends. Last year, her seventh-grade friend Isabel, who lived in Yonhi Manor, had brought back three of them. She kept one and gave the other two to her next-door neighbors, Ester and Sarah. Isabel said the *mapes* would symbolize that they were to be FRIENDS FOREVER! Everybody around school knew that was the truth. Those three girls always tried to dress alike, wear the same shoes, and they even wore their hair in the same style! Their identical *mape* key chains hung from the zippers on their book bags, along with a collection of other clattery key chains of various Disney characters, a seahorse shape from the COEX aquarium, and three tiny soccer balls.

Later that afternoon, Claire walked down the Pig Path, an old dirt footpath that wound behind the apartment houses, toward Isabel's house.

**The pig path**

Isabel's mother Luanne was Claire's piano teacher. As she neared the front gate, she noticed a police car was parked in front of the house. She hesitated for a moment as Isabel's mom stepped out the door, followed by two policemen. The police officers got into their car, and Isabel's mother beckoned for Claire to come in.

"What was that all about?" asked Claire.

"They were just following up on all the robberies that have taken place around here during the past several months. All of the homes seem to be where school families live, so the police think there is some connection with Seoul Foreign School.

"YIKES!" burst out Claire. "I sure hope they don't find connections to our family! My mom and dad work there!"

"So far," Isabel's mom explained, "the homes where the robbers entered were only located in the Yonhi Manor compound. No robberies have ever been reported on the Seoul Foreign School compound."

# 3.

# All Aboard!

**M**onday morning arrived. Mr. Van used his checklist to verify that each of the sixth-grade students had submitted their parental permission slips, their travel documents and their fees. He cross-checked his lists to see that all address and phone numbers were accurate. Finally, he called down to the school nurse to see if any of the children had any special health concerns that he needed to know about. All of the airline tickets were in his briefcase. Everything seemed to be in order for the trip on Tuesday. He contacted the activities director to make sure that the buses were reserved for the trip to the old airport. They would be using the old Gimpo airport, not the new Inchon International Airport, since the trip to Cheju-do would be a domestic flight.

The chaperones were in and out all day, checking on the final details. Mr. Goneway, the principal, smiled in approval as he observed another popular field trip take shape. He delivered one of the school's digital cameras, a cell phone, and a laptop computer to Mr. Van's classroom. "It looks like you have everything under control!" he said, with an encouraging smile.

"I think we are ready now," replied Mr. Van.

Tuesday morning finally spread across South Korea, the nation with the beautiful nickname, "The Land of the Morning Calm." However, the bus loading area was anything but calm. It was alive with chattering people of all ages, huge motor coaches, long rows of suitcases, bags, and backpacks.

"Where's my bag?" yelled Jack, as he ran toward the bus. He had been playing soccer on the playground. It was his favorite thing to do before the morning bell rang.

"Right where you left it!" called Steve. "See it over there, on the edge of the soccer field!" Jack hurried off to get it as excited boys and girls began to fill the buses. Returning to the loading area, Jack put his bags with the others and joined his friends as they hopped into their assigned bus.

Finally, the bus doors closed. As the huge vehicles rolled toward the driveway a long column of teachers, parents, and children waved their goodbyes and threw kisses toward the moving vehicles.

High in the tree, Yazdee watched with great curiosity. Craning her neck first one way and then the other, she attempted to get a better view. Satisfied that she had not missed a thing, she lifted herself from her nest and gently turned her eggs. Then, with a quick forward lunge, she took to the air in search of food. While gliding in a wider circle, she spotted Tigger down below. He had already bagged his morning catch, a plump mouse from behind the flower pot on Mrs. Solee's deck. The cat was on his way back to the F building to deposit it at the side of the main entrance. Yazdee had watched him do this before. He placed his latest prize near a small mound of treasures he had collected under the leaves near a tree by the fence.

The magpie flock to which Yazdee belonged was average in size. Their feeding area included all of Yonhi Dong. It was bound by the major roads that led from the Swiss Grande Hotel to the intersection of the street toward Yonsi University. It included a meandering road that cut through the university campus and connected to the hospital. The whole area was a hungry bird's paradise, including a ready supply of garbage dumpsters and surrounding litter dropped by thousands of people who daily walked these streets. Yazdee scrounged freely, satisfied her hunger and eventually ascended back to her nest.

# 4.

# Cheju-do! Here We Come!

The flight to Cheju-do went as scheduled. As the Asiana Carrier neared the island, excitement began to rise. Nearly all of the seats on the plane were occupied by the sixth-grade class. The teachers, Mr. Bill, Miss Roxie, and Mr. Van, along with nine parents accompanied sixty boys and girls on this trip. Those with window seats leaned close to get a better view as the south-bound plane lowered over the ocean surface and lined up for a perfect landing on the island's airstrip.

"I see palm trees!" yelled Steve.

"Look! A McDonald's and a Wendy's!" added Brian.

"Look! I see my mother! Just kidding!" teased Jack.

A loud cheer and applause filled the cabin as the seat belt sign was turned off. Popping open their seatbelts, the excited students loudly erupted into the aisles.

Once the luggage was accounted for, the group headed toward the buses waiting to take them to their hotel. "Look at those huge propellers! What are they for?" asked Steve, who was seated behind Mr. Bill.

"Those are windmills. They generate over 5% of all the electricity used in South Korea. Remember when we did our inquiry unit on 'Let's Get Power?' Well! Here is an example of an alternative to petroleum as a source for energy. God already provides the wind. We just need to use it. Last year, our tour guide explained that Cheju Island is known for wind, women and rocks. It has an abundance of all three!"

"That's cool," added Craig, who was listening. "I wonder how much electricity could be generated by other windy places around the globe!"

Jack asked, "Why do you sometimes say 'Cheju' and other times say 'Cheju-do' when you talk about the island?"

"That's because in the Korean language, 'do' means island," replied Mr. Bill.

Their curiosity satisfied for the time being, the boys settled back into their seats.

"Wow! Look at those palm trees! We don't have anything like that in Seoul!" shouted Claire.

Miss Roxie replied, "Cheju-do is called 'The Hawaii of Korea.' Usually it is warmer and sunnier here. That's why the island is also the place many newlyweds choose for their honeymoon."

**The Hawaii of Korea**

Claire and Annie rolled their eyes and giggled. Steve and Jack just sighed loudly and continued to look out the window of the bus.

When they reached the Oriental Hotel, Mr. Van took care of the check-in details and distributed the room keys. "Take your things to your rooms. Get your buffet lunch in the dining room, and then come back here at one o'clock." Following several trips using the elevator, the luggage at the front entrance was eventually sorted out and delivered to the correct rooms.

"Listen up!" Promptly at 1 pm Mr. Van handed out the tour brochures. For the rest of the afternoon, they would tour a museum, take a bus tour of this area of the island, and end the day with a buffet meal at the Crown Restaurant. They boarded the buses and began their adventure.

Exhibits at the museum explained the volcanic remains of the island. The boys were fascinated by a huge stuffed fish in the middle of the room. Fishermen from the island had caught it many years ago. It was as big as a small submarine! They were also kept busy with a large interactive map with headphones attached. When they pushed a button for certain location, a tiny bulb would light up and information about that place could be heard through the headphones.

"Did you hear that Cheju-do has secret caves where pirates used to hide?" whispered Steve. "Look! They are shown here on the map!"

"Yes!" answered Mark. "I hope we get to see those caves!"

The girls marveled at the exhibit featuring the work of the women on the island. History books say that because the men on the island spent much time out at sea, the women had to find ways to support themselves and their children. Many of them learned how to dive for pearls and other marine life deep in the sea. Dressed in black rubber suits, flippers, and goggles, and while carrying nets and fishing baskets, they spent their days diving into the ocean in search of pearl-filled clams, hoping to sell the gems. To this day, women on the island continue to dive for pearls.

Miss Roxie showed the girls the exhibit about Mongolian horses that had been brought to the island by the Chinese warlord, Genghis Khan in the year 1275. At that time Cheju–do was used as a headquarters by his army in a war against Japan. Today, not many of these horses remain. In order to help maintain the tiny horse population, the Cheju ponies race on weekends to pay for their upkeep. The exhibit explained that the ponies come in a variety of colors, which certainly makes it easy to pick your pony from the crowd! "I think you will enjoy seeing the large herds of horses on this island," she said.

"Oh! I love horses!" replied Claire. "My uncle has horses on his farm in Iowa!"

"Hey! Annie said, "Let's all make a wish every time we see a white horse. Okay?"

The other girls agreed. They continued to walk around the museum and write comments in their journals until Mr. Van signaled that it was time to get back to the bus.

The tour guide explained that the objects spread along the sides of the road were green onions being dried for planting next year. The island produces green onions of the highest quality. They are sold in markets all over South Korea. She also said that this area is noted for producing Seaweed Jelly, a delicacy enjoyed by many Korean people.

Pointing toward a strange-looking scene, she said, "Be sure to take note of the tan-colored objects hanging on those fences over there. That is ocean squid which has been hung up to dry. You will find dried squid later at the fish market.

"We are now approaching Sunrise Peak," announced the tour guide. "Notice the color of the water as it ranges from soft green to aqua off the coastline. A small coral reef surrounds this peninsula.

After the bus was parked, the classes began to follow a footpath up toward the peak. Off in a distance, a trail wound through the field where horse-back rides were offered for a price.

"I see a white horse!" shouted Annie. The girls made their first wish.

**Make a wish!**

The group continued along the path and then took a side trail that overlooked a small cove. A giant outcrop of rocks resembled chunks of petrified Swiss cheese. Sharp crevices, small caves, and tiny holes covered the surface. It had been formed by years of ocean waves and strong winds pounding the island.

The main trail to the peak was long and steep. Some children were content to sit on benches and enjoy the scenery. Jack led a small pack of kids who raced to the top.

Breathless from the walk, Mr. Bill arrived at the peak several minutes later. He used the video recorder to capture expressions of the students who had reached the end of the path. They held up two fingers in a V for Victory pose. Behind them a white, black, red, and blue South Korean flag fluttered in the wind.

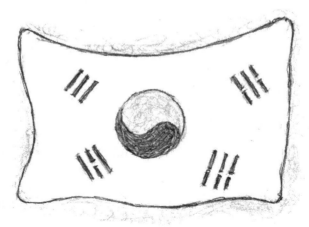

*The flag of South Korea*

Jack and Craig purchased small pieces of volcanic rock that had been carved into turtles, fish, and other sea animals. These black rocks were full of tiny holes and amazingly light-weight for their size.

Everyone was hungry as the group entered the Crown Dining Room for dinner.

"'*Kim*' means seaweed and '*Bap*' means rice. Those were my first words for food in Korean," explained Annie as they munched on their *Kim-Bap* appetizers. Their dinner also featured *Kimchi* (marinated cabbage) *pibimbap* (hot rice with vegetables,) rice cakes, and persimmon punch. After the meal, they returned to the hotel and settled down for the night.

# 5.

# So Much to See!

The next morning, Mr. Van announced the plans for the day. "Today we will visit the folk village, have our lunch there, and if the weather is good, we will hire a ferry boat to cruise around the outside of the island to see the Chong-ji-yon Waterfalls. They can only be seen from the sea." The last item brought excited responses from the boys. They had heard that the pirate's caves were in that same area.

The folk village was an interesting place. The workers wore rust-colored costumes. A tour guide explained that hemp fabric had been treated with an ancient process. It was soaked in persimmon tea to give it that soft brownish color. This absorbent fabric holds up well even when workers are hot and sweaty.

Folk artists demonstrated crafts using methods and processes practiced by their ancestors. The exhibitors worked in cottages with thatched roofs and dirt floors. Following Korean tradition, pumpkin vines had been trained to climb to the rooftops, where plump orange pumpkins with curly tendrils peeked out between huge green leaves. Brightly colored flowers, neatly trimmed shrubs and budding Ginkgo trees lined the walking paths.

*Pumpkin vines climbed to the rooftops*

The students were encouraged to participate and produce their own samples of wood carving, calligraphy, jewelry, baskets, candles, stitchery, paper, and simple kites.

A special treat was a sample of peanut candy from the traditional candy vendor. He sliced off chunks of the chewy sweets with an over-sized metal shears that hung from a hook on the side of his food cart.

One area demonstrated the Korean custom of wrapping tree trunks. This ancient practice is still performed in late fall to prepare the trees for the winter season. Straw mats are attached to the trunks of trees.

***Wrapped tree trunks***

The idea is that pests will nest in these mats and lay their eggs. In early spring, the mats are removed and burned, destroying the pests and their larvae. Sometimes entire bushes are enclosed in straw wrapping for the winter season.

Another stall was filled with hand-made musical instruments. A man demonstrated the process of heating amber resin to a high temperature to produce a fine liquid varnish. This rich yellow substance is used to create a long-lasting shiny finish on violins and other stringed instruments.

An interesting method for villagers to leave messages was explained by the tour guide. A *Chung non* gate was used for this purpose. Three wooden poles rested beside the gate. If the gate opening was barred by one pole, it meant that the occupant of the cottage would be gone for about 10 minutes. If two poles barred the gate, it meant that the cottage owner was out in the field. Three poles barring the gate meant that the owner would be gone for a week or longer.

At an outdoor theater area, a traditional Korean wedding ceremony was portrayed by a drama troupe. The entire cast wore elaborate costumes. The men wore pajama-like suits of colorful silk with matching hats and boots. Their baggy pants were tied at the ankles.

The bride was dressed in a billowing *hanbok* of bright red and yellow silk. Rows of shimmering gold threads edged the toe-length skirt. A knotted bow with a jeweled tassel decorated the jacket. Her attendants wore similar costumes in vibrant contrasting colors. Their sparkling head-dresses, bracelets, and necklaces glittered with gold and semi-precious stones.

To show respect and submission to her future husband, the bride kept her head lowered and partially hidden behind a long piece of white cloth that her attendants held in front of her face.

"Look at that head piece," giggled Claire. "If I wore something like that on my head, I would have a big headache!"

"Yes, but you would wear it for only a few hours," whispered Annie.

"I think it would be fun just to try it on," added Emily.

Mr. Bill moved slowly around the edge of the crowd as he continued to refocus for close-up photos with the digital camera.

The formal ceremony began with the groom and his two attendant's arrival on white horses. The bride was carried to the stage in an ornate wooden box with veiled windows. The ceremonial ritual included deep formal bows by the bride and groom to both sets of parents. It took place on a thatched mat with a black lacquer table at the center of the stage. Among other items on the table was a basket with a pair of live ducks. Following Korean tradition, these wedding ducks were to symbolize everlasting married love.

Afterwards, Emily asked Claire and Annie if they had made three more wishes when they spotted the three white horses in the wedding ceremony. "Cool!" they all agreed.

Another highlight was a drumming performance by the *Nong-ak* drumming troupe. They wore simple white and black costumes, cloth boots and hats with a ribbon attached at the top. By rapidly twisting their heads in circular motions, they could make the ribbons whiz around in wide circles above their heads. What energy! What deafening rhythms! What skill they showed in their elaborate movements as they danced around the stage with dizzying leaps and twirls as they continued to wildly drum!

# 6.

# Taste of Korea

Lunch was served at a large concrete area with raised wooden platforms. On each platform was a low table. Customers knelt on woven floor mats around each table as the food was served. On this day the special feature was *Pajeon*, a traditional crispy Korean pancake filled with green onions. Small dipping dishes at each place were filled with a mixture of soy sauce and vinegar. *Kim-Bap*, fresh oranges and persimmon tea completed the meal.

Following the meal, they visited the gift shop. The boys admired black and white chess boards made from sun-bleached stones and volcanic rock.

The playing pieces were carved from various shades of green jade. The girls were interested in finding souvenir *mape* medallions. They found a few, but decided to wait and see if they could find some that were not so expensive.

Miss Roxie decided to buy a small black jewelry box. The top of the box was inlaid with shiny pieces of mother-of-pearl in soft rainbow colors. Inside were a mirror and a tiny ballerina dancer who twirled when you wound the key on the bottom of the box.

Soon it was time for the group to make their way back to the buses in the parking lot.

As the buses rolled through the countryside, herds of cattle and horses grazed in the fields. The landscape was so different from the busy city of Seoul. Small but tidy garden plots were separated by low walls built from tightly stacked stones and rocks. Orange groves and fields of pineapple plants were tended by workers who walked from their homes in surrounding villages.

As the bus turned off the main road and headed toward the boat launch, Claire pointed toward another white horse in the distance. The girls closed their eyes and made their wishes.

Mr. Van purchased the tickets for the ferry at the marine office as the group gathered at the edge of the dock. When given directions to board the ferry, they excitedly lined up and made their way out to the end of the dock.

Always in a hurry, Jack pushed around the edge of the group and nearly fell over the side. Pulling the boy toward him, Mr. Bill reminded everyone to wear the life jackets provided for each passenger, which were under the seats.

Finally they were moving. "I hope I don't get seasick," murmured Annie.

"You won't," said Claire. "Just keep your eyes focused on something far away. Besides, it is a really calm day today, thank goodness!" Emily dug around in her purse to find some gum for her friends.

Resembling a huge glass box on the main deck of the ferry, the seating area was enclosed with windows. Tables and booths were built in front of the windows, and rows of beach chairs filled the center area. Hot noodle soup, seaweed snacks, peanut candies, and soft drinks were sold at a food stall at one end of the room. "I wish they would give out forks with the noodles," Annie commented, as the girls slurped the soup they had purchased. "I have never been able to figure out how to eat noodle soup with chopsticks!" The other girls giggled and nodded in agreement.

Sounding like a small airplane, the ferry boat cut through the water, following the contour of the island. "Oh rats!" Emily had checked out the rest rooms and discovered that they were "squatty potties." This meant there were no western-type toilets. Instead, the potty was basically a porcelain hole in the floor with no flushing mechanism. To use it, you had to stand facing the closed door of the stall, place your feet on the bricks on each side of the hole, squat, and do your business, clean your bottom, and deposit the toilet tissue in the waste basket.

A bucket of water with a dipper was provided to clean the potty after use. It usually took several dippers full of water to flush the contents of the toilet bowl into the holding tank below the potty. Knowing that bathroom tissue was not always supplied in these rest rooms, the girls always kept extra packets of Kleenex in their bags.

A few minutes later, Jack and Craig appeared beside the girl's booth. "Umm...do you have any Kleenex?"

The girls just giggled. "Yes, for 2000 *won*," piped up Claire.

"That's robbery!...1000!" Jack shouted back.

"Okay, okay. 1000!" Claire said, as she opened her backpack and tossed a Kleenex packet to him. "Bring your own next time!"

"My brother is just like that," sighed Annie. "So irresponsible."

# 7.

# Floating Market

As the ferry glided around the point of a peninsula, a grotto-like cove and the Chon-ji-yon Waterfalls came into view. Steep rugged cliffs edged the massive waterfall. Ocean spray rose from below, where the churning waters crashed and rumbled. Rainbow colors peeked through the misty air. Guarding the area, moss-covered rocks with jagged edges rose knifelike from the water. The ferry slowed as it neared the scene, carefully dodging underwater coral beds and sharp-edged rock formations. Everyone focused their cameras for a snapshot of this spectacular sight.

By this time, nearly everyone had come out of the viewing room. They were standing side by side and holding unto the ferry railing. "Look!" shouted Jack. "Pirate's caves! Here, there and over there! Wow! I wonder if they left any treasures buried inside."

***Pirate's caves!***

As he pointed toward the caves, three men in a shiny white speedboat came into view. Nearing the ferry, the driver cut the engine and the boat glided to a stop. The captain of the ferry waved and greeted the men. For a short time, the two boats heaved and tossed side by side in the water. Eventually, a connecting rope from the speedboat was tossed over a post on the ferry railing, and one of the men climbed aboard.

The captain of the ferry smiled widely and introduced Mee Happee to Mr. Van. The captain invited the group to check out the items for sale at the back of the speed boat. "This is a service we provide with all of our tours," he said.

"OK SOOVINEERS" was painted in shiny black letters on the side of the boat. Racks with a variety of souvenirs hung from parallel bars at the rear of the boat. Costumed dolls, tiny silk bags with colorful strips, pendants on chains, fancy hair combs, small stuffed animals, key chains with decorative attachments, calendars, painted scrolls, and cheap tee shirts hung on racks. Boxes on the floor were filled with large candy bars and other tempting snacks that were different from those stocked on the ferry.

## *OK SOOVINEERS*

Several students reached for their wallets and coin purses as they pointed toward items they wanted to buy. For the next twenty minutes the two men on the boat happily conducted their business on their miniature floating market as Mee Happee climbed over and back across to the railing to deliver items to the customers on the ferry.

"Hey, look!" shouted Annie. "They sell *mapes* with six horses, and they cost only half as much as the same kind we saw back in the gift shop!" The girls each eagerly exchanged their money for several *mapes*. "One of my wishes has come true," squealed Annie!

It was late afternoon when the ferry reached the boat launch area. Everyone was hungry again and they were also looking forward to a good night's sleep. They found a good price for food at the Burger King near the hotel. They topped off the meal with ice cream cones from a shop nearby. The boys took a poll and determined that the two top flavors were peanut butter chocolate caramel and butter pecan.

When they reached the hotel, Mr. Van explained that everyone needed to have their bags ready in the morning when they came to breakfast. The luggage was to be loaded on the buses. Their return flight to Seoul was scheduled just before noon.

# 8.

# Returning Home

The morning passed quickly. After breakfast in the hotel coffee shop, they visited the Wood and Stone Garden. Here, artists used wood and stone to interpret legends of the island of Cheju. The scent of sandalwood filled the air. Vendors displayed hand fans, gift boxes, and various other items carved from this fragrant wood. Jack bought a tiny box carved from sandalwood. It contained a life-sized cricket made of straw. The box was cleverly made. When it was opened, the man-made cricket chirped!

Annie bought an interesting pendant. Inside the first round sphere was an identical smaller ball. Each sphere was intricately carved from sandalwood. The tiny sphere on the inside could move independently from the outer one.

Several of the mothers purchased folding hand fans made from paper-thin slats of scented sandalwood. Miss Roxie bought a hand-painted umbrella with a beautifully carved sandalwood handle.

Later they experienced the Illusion Road. It is a 100-meter strip where the road is slightly sloped, causing one to believe that you are rolling in the opposite direction. "That was weird!" exclaimed Jack, as they drove on.

"I just saw another white horse! Make a wish!" Claire called out as she pointed toward the herd of horses grazing beside the road.

The last stop on the tour was the amethyst factory. Everything at this place was very expensive, but it was interesting to hear how the beautiful purple amethyst was mined and made into jewelry. Gemstones such as rubies, emeralds, and diamonds were also displayed in the glass showcases that were lined in black velvet. The guide explained that amethyst may lose its brilliance if exposed to direct sunlight, so black velvet and dark cloth is used to protect these jewels. The boys watched as Mr. Van purchased a fine golden chain with an amethyst pendant to take home to his wife.

Finally, the buses were packed and headed for the airport. The flight to Seoul was uneventful, a blessing for which all were thankful.

Back at SFS, the sixth-graders tumbled from the buses, hugged their waiting families, and gathered their bags and bundles. They were a tired but talkative crowd.

Yazdee was pleased to see their return. A rainstorm was approaching, and she hoped they would make it to their homes before the downpour.

Later that afternoon, the magpie watched as a noisy motorcycle roared up the hill. A *WE DO PIZZA* box was attached behind the driver's seat. Admitted by the security guards, the vehicle entered the Yohni Manor compound. Slowly moving through the complex, it made two rounds and then drove out through the gate and down the hill.

**WE DO PIZZA**

Attracted by a sparkle from the from the driver's helmet, Yazdee remembered this vehicle on following days as it made trips through the compound. One afternoon the bird squawked loudly when she saw its wheels narrowly miss Tigger! The cat was running while carrying something shiny in his mouth. "That cat is up to no good, as usual," thought the bird.

Yazdee screeched and cackled to share her daily observations with the other magpies as they swarmed each evening at dusk. Ignoring her, the birds flapped and fluttered higher to catch their ride on the evening currents. Dipping and soaring, they circled for many minutes. Having stretched their wings in this final daily ritual, they settled into their nests and quieted down for the night. Now after sundown, a cuckoo called from the trees farther up the hill.

# 9.

# Robberies!

The following morning a police car arrived at Yonhi Manor. Mrs. Brown was missing her emerald earrings and a sting of pearls. The window in the bathroom was open, and the ornaments on the shelf below were knocked over. Two gold Krugerrand coins were missing from the Jensen's home. Their back door was standing open. Anne Ford's diamond and ruby ring had disappeared. Behind the drapes, an SFS yearbook was propped into the sliding door to prevent it from closing.

The security guards were questioned. They had seen nothing uncommon. The normal people had checked in and out at the gate. All of the delivery people had provided the correct identification badges. The guards promised to be more diligent. The police would continue to investigate.

That morning, Mr. Van's classroom was louder than usual.

"Did you hear?" asked Craig. "We were robbed!"

"What!! So were we!" shrieked Steve.

"Hey! Us too!" chimed in Brian.

"My mom said not to be scared, but I am," Claire murmured in a low voice as she wrapped her arms tightly around her book bag.

"Well, the police are on it." Craig tried to be calm.

"Yeah, but they don't LIVE in this neighborhood!" wailed Annie. "It makes me feel creepy to think that the thief knows when we are home and when we are out. Imagine! I wouldn't want anybody pawing through my private stuff, either!"

Brian suddenly burst out, "Hey! Maybe we could try to crack the case! Look, all of the families were school families. They all have kids in the sixth-grade."

"What are you trying to suggest? Do you think the robber is one of us?" asked Claire.

"No, not that!" said Brian. "Let's see if there are any other clues. Let's make a list."

1. All robberies have been in Yonhi Manor.
2. All who were robbed were school families.
3. All who were robbed have kids in grade six.

"Any other clues?" asked Steve.

"I can't think of any," replied Jack.

"When did the robberies take place?" Brian asked.

Jack quickly raised his hand, as though he had come up with a bright idea. "Hey, they all happened after the sixth-grade trip, just like last year, when Gloria's mom had her amethyst chess set stolen. Remember, that was right after the sixth-grade trip, too!"

Brian clicked his pen and began to write. "Let's put that down as our fourth clue. All robberies took place after the sixth-grade class trip to Cheju-do."

"Hey, everybody," said Jack. If you want to work some more on this, come to my place after school!"

# 10.

# Campus Cats

At three-thirty, several kids from the class gathered on the steps behind the E building. Brian unfolded the paper with the list of clues, and everybody started to talk at once. "Okay, okay, one at a time," he said, as he raised both hands.

"I think we need to start watching the gate at Yonhi Manor," suggested Emily. "To get in there, you need to go through the gate."

"But the guards already watch the gate," replied Jack.

"Well then," said Brian, "maybe we need to start watching the guards."

The group decided to move over to the trees near the F building. Peeking from behind a tree, Brian said, "Let's just stay here for awhile and watch to see if those guards are really doing their job."

"Look!" whispered Annie. "One is opening the gate right now!" They watched as another guard wrote down the license number of the car that moved though the gate. The guards repeated this process several times as more cars entered the compound.

Once, they saw a delivery man approach on a motorbike from *WE DO PIZZA*. He held up his identification badge, and the security guard waved him through the gate. When he came out several minutes later, they noticed that his front tire narrowly missed a large gray cat. The cat had hopped from the bushes with something shiny in its mouth. Startled by the noise, the cat jumped aside and then raced behind the motorbike through the gate.

"That's Tigger, Mr. Van's cat!" shouted Jack. "It's a good thing that cats have nine lives!"

They continued to watch. The guards seemed to do their jobs as expected for the next hour or so. It became boring. Convinced that nothing looked unusual, the boys and girls decided they would stop watching for now and meet on another day to decided what to do next.

Before they went home, the girls walked up the long driveway to a square stone house at the top of the hill. A retired missionary named Aunt Rose lived there. She was a friend of all the families who lived on the SFS compound. She was like a grandmother to all of them. Her house had shiny wooden floors. She kept colorful cloth slippers by her front door for visitors to wear after they had removed their street shoes and put them on the shoe rack. The girls loved to visit her because she always invited them in for snacks and shared interesting stories. They also liked to play with her two cats. Sultan was a long-legged gray Persian with deep blue eyes. Queenie was a pure white Angora with green eyes.

**Sultan and Queenie**

Today the girls planned to give Aunt Rose a *mape* souvenir they brought back from Cheju-do. "Thank you! How kind of you to think of me! I have several key chains, but I have never had one like this," Aunt Rose said as she attached the key chain to her large tote bag. The girls explained that they chose the *mape* with six horses because according to Korean legends, it was the most special, and they wanted her to know that she was special to them. They visited for a few more minutes until it was time for the girls to go home.

# 11.

# Lesson from a Pearl

It was a new day, and Mr. Van was ready to begin with morning devotions. He quietly stood at the front of the room with his hand raised. Soon the students quieted down and silently took their seats. Reaching for his guitar, he began strumming the chords to "Allelu, Allelu." Everyone joined to sing along with this praise song. It was one of their favorites.

Following the song, he asked the class to think about things they had seen while on their class trip to Cheju-do. As the boys and girls mentioned various memories, he listed their ideas on the white board.

Then he circled one of the ideas on the list...PEARL DIVERS. "I think we can learn something from the experience of a pearl," he said.

Claire turned and smiled at Emily. Then she looked back at her teacher. She loved it when he explained truths from the Bible by connecting them with familiar objects.

Mr. Van explained that a pearl is formed when a speck of sand or some other foreign particle becomes trapped inside a seashell. To protect itself, the live mollusk inside the shell excretes a sticky fluid coating over the speck to make it slippery and less irritable. As time passes, the mollusk continues to wash the speck in this sticky fluid, causing the speck to grow in size, layer by layer, until a beautiful pearly gem is formed within the seashell. Just like the pearl divers on Cheju-do, people around the world hunt for these special seashells. Beautiful pearls are removed from the shells and offered to the world as precious treasures.

**A Lesson From a Pearl**

Mr. Van explained, "It is possible for each of us to experience a similar miracle in our lives. Because we sin, harmful habits or behaviors try to settle inside us, just like a speck of sand gets into a sea-shell. Without help, we might be seriously damaged or even destroyed. The good news is that God has a way for us to deal with this problem. With His help, it is possible to replace bad habits and behaviors with good growth. The Bible tells us that God's love for us never stops. Layer upon layer, He continues to wash us over and over with His forgiveness, His hope and His promises. As we learn more of His plans for us and begin to trust Him to work within us, our attitudes and behaviors can positively change. We might then take on a new brilliance and begin to glow with new life. Just as the ordinary speck of sand becomes a shimmering pearl, our sinful habits and behaviors can be overcome by God's mercy, transforming us into His precious treasures, glowing with His love. During our Bible class today we will study what Jesus did for us so that we can experience this miracle."

Blond-haired Steve wondered where Mr. Van had learned to think like that. "He can take the most ordinary object and connect it to some idea about God!"

Tardy today, Annie charged through the door with her book bag slung over one shoulder. As she swung it around to take it off, her new *mape* keychain hit the corner of a desk and snapped off. As it hit the floor it broke into pieces.

"Hey! Look at that!" Steve said as he pointed to the floor.

"What?" asked Annie.

"That thing from inside your *mape*. It looks like a tiny microchip!"

Mr. Van walked down the aisle to take a look. "You're right. It does look like a microchip."

"Why would there be a microchip inside this cheap souvenir?" she wondered.

"I don't know, but maybe we should try to find out," replied Mr. Van.

After examining the microchip from the *mape* key chain on Annie's bag, Mr. Van asked to see the key chains other students had bought from the men on the flashy speed boat. Carefully taking them apart, he discovered that each one contained a tiny blue microchip.

With a concerned look he said, "This is very strange!"

Everyone started to talk at once. "Hang on!" Mr. Van said. "Let's try to figure this out."

With a puzzled expression on his face, Brian asked, "Why would somebody go through the trouble to implant a microchip in each of these things and then sell them so cheaply?"

"Yes that is strange," answered Mr. Van. "Now let's think. What are microchips, and for what are they used?"

"I know," said Jack as he raised his hand and talked at the same time. "Let's Google it and see what we find out!"

"Why don't you use that as your independent project today in computer class," suggested Mr. Van.

"Okay! Can Steve and Brian work with me?"

"That's fine," answered Mr. Van. "Plan to tell us what you've discovered during tomorrow's computer class."

# 12.

# Computer Research

In the computer lab, the three boys gathered around Jack's computer. Jack keyed in the words "uses for microchip." A list of several websites popped up. The boys chose four sites and studied them for information. Gathering ideas from each source, they came up with a list of several ways microchips can be used. They typed the list, recorded their sources, and saved the file in Microsoft Word.

At the end of their lesson on the following day, Mr. Van asked the boys to download their work and project it unto the overhead screen so the whole class could view their notes. Jack explained their work.

Their report found that microchips can be used in computers, guided missiles, "smart bombs," satellites, television, communication devices, aircraft, spacecraft, motor vehicles, identification tags, and games. They were prepared to explain with more details, but another class needed to use the lab, so the sixth-graders had to close their programs and leave.

They continued the discussion in the classroom. "Which of these uses might seem to be right for these souvenirs?" asked Mr. Van.

"I hope they aren't intelligent bombs," Claire said in a shaky voice.

"'Smart bombs,'" corrected Brian. "No, I don't think the little key chains are sophisticated enough for anything like that, and obviously, several things on that list don't seem likely. For example, we didn't buy any computers, guided missiles, televisions, satellites, aircraft, or spacecraft."

"More likely, the key chains could be used as identification devices, like microchips attached to

ID tags of pets to locate them if they are missing," suggested Jack.

"Hey, maybe that's it! Maybe they were trying to trace how far their souvenirs were being carried! Maybe it is part of their market research!" exclaimed Emily.

At recess, Mr. Van noticed Aunt Rose had walked down from her home on the hill. She was talking with one of the SFS security guards. Eventually, all of them walked into the school building.

At the teachers' meeting after school Mr. Goneway told the faculty that a new theft had taken place. For the first time, it was on the SFS school property. He said Aunt Rose was missing some things from her jewelry box. She wasn't sure, but she thought it may have happened the night before while she was at a meeting. She had propped the back door open with a brick so the cats could go in or out.

# 13.

# Cracking the Case

The following morning, the classroom buzzed with news about the new burglary. Bits of conversation mingled with confusion. "Aunt Rose's house...jewelry...scared cats behind the sofa...she was gone...who did it?" The sixth-grade detectives decided to meet again at Jack's place after school.

"Okay," Brain said as he pulled the paper with the clues from his back pocket. "The first three clues no longer are true. NOT all the robberies were at Yonhi Manor. NOT all the robbed families were from Seoul Foreign School. NOT all the robbed families had sixth-graders. The only clue that is still useful is that the robberies took place after the trip to Cheju-do. We've got to come up with some better clues, you guys."

"But Aunt Rose was robbed, and she didn't have anything t do with our trip to Cheju-do," said Annie. As soon as the words came out of her mouth, she froze. "Wait a minute!" she exchanged looks with Claire and Emily. They seem to know exactly what she was thinking.

"Yes! That's it!" All three girls shouted together.

"Remember when we walked up to her house and gave her that souvenir from our trip?" said Annie.

"Yes! It was just like ours, a *mape* with six horses!" added Emily. "And it probably has a microchip, too!"

"Hey, maybe Aunt Rose can help us," suggested Annie.

The group decided to walk up the hill to her house and ask her some questions. As they came closer, they could see that she was on the porch. She greeted them and explained that she had been watching the magpies as they circled above.

"They flock like this every evening just before sundown," she said. "Although tonight it looks like they are flying closer to the buildings. In fact, one nearly came through my bedroom window! It hit the screen with a loud thud! I came out here to see if it was okay. It's not around, so I think it must be up there again with all the rest of them."

Brian asked if she had some time to talk. She asked them to come in, so they took off their shoes and followed her into the small living room.

Brian spoke up for the group. "We think we might have a clue about the robbery."

"Oh good," she said. "The police have been working on it, but they have not reported anything new yet."

'We think there might be some connection between your robbery and the *mape* key chain the girls gave to you. What do you think?" he asked.

"Well, that is possible, but how could we figure that out?" she asked.

"What did you do with the key chain when the girls gave it to you?" asked Brain.

"See here," she said, as she showed them the key chain as it dangled from the strap on her hand bag. "I attached it right away."

"You mean it was attached to your bag all the time, even when you were out of the house?" he asked.

"Of course," said Aunt Rose.

"Well, that's it! The microchip inside the key chain must be able to track your movements. Somebody must be tracking you, Aunt Rose!"

"OH! THIS IS TOO SCARY!" wailed Claire.

"Wait a minute! If someone was tracking you and could figure out when you we not in the house, is there any we can figure out who that might be?" asked Steve. "Think, Aunt Rose. Who has been up here lately?"

"Well, nobody unusual, that I can think of. Everybody had to pass through the security gate down at the bottom of the hill, anyway," she said.

"Well, that is true, but maybe the suspect could be somebody that was allowed to pass or somebody who passed without being noticed."

"Oh! I didn't think of that," she said. "Let me see. Well, there are the usual teachers who live up here. They come and go all the time. Then, of course, the security guards walk around each building and key in at all the check-locks several times each day. Sometimes that gray cat of Mr. Van's follows them along their route. My cats don't get along with that one, though. They hide when they see him around here. That's about all, I think. Oh, the pizza delivery man delivers up here, too, once a week or so."

"From the Chicago Pizza place down by the main road?" Brian asked.

"No, from the *WE DO PIZZA*," she answered. "You know, that nice young man with the shiny helmet and flashy designs on his motorbike."

"That's interesting," Brian replied. "I suppose the pizza guys have the right identification to get through the security gate. But, they would need to know if you are home or not in order to deliver the pizza."

Suddenly Annie had an idea! "What if the pizza man had a way to know when somebody was NOT at home? He could still pretend he was delivering a pizza. He could get through the security gate and into somebody's place without any problem!"

The room became very quiet. YES! That had to be it! Then everyone started to talk at once!

Finally, Brian asked Aunt Rose if they could borrow her *mape* key chain. They wanted to show it to Mr. Van. She removed it from her bag and gave it to him. They boys and girls thanked Aunt Rose and ran back to the school building to see if Mr. Van was still there. He was in his classroom talking with Mr. Bill as they all pushed through the door.

"We think we might have cracked the case!" shouted Brian, as everyone tried to talk at once.

"Slow down! One at a time!" Brian told him about everything – the meeting, the clues, Aunt Rose and her key chain, and finally, their suspicions about the pizza delivery man.

Mr. Van took a deep breath and reached into his pocket for his cell phone. "These are very good leads. I think we need to share your ideas with the police."

# 14.

# Crafty Technology

The following days were exciting! The newspapers and TV hailed it as a major discovery! A massive theft on the South Korean peninsula had been broken!

A week later, the police chief was in the sixth-grade classroom. He was there to explain how the sixth-grade trip had a major connection with the case.

What a break through! The police were able to trace the microchips to a company run by the same people who worked for the boat launch in Cheju-do. In fact, the police had been keeping an eye on this group for a couple of years. However, they had never been able to pin them down with any solid evidence.

Evidently, with the use of the microchips embedded in the small key chains, the theft ring was able to trace the daily habits of the individuals using the key chains. Of special importance were two styles of key chains. Those inscribed with the words *To My Mom* or those designed with six horses were sold only to students from the sixth-grade at Seoul Foreign School.

When the police closed in on the company in Cheju-do, they found three men they had been tracking for two years in the Yonhi Dong area. When questioned, the men admitted their connection to the robberies in the Yonhi Manor compound. In fact, among the items confiscated by the police were 2 golden Kruggerand coins, a pearl necklace, and an amethyst chess set.

One of the suspects was wearing a silk jacket embossed with the words "*We Do Pizza.*"

Under intense questioning, he admitted to masterminding all of the robberies at Yonhi Manor. He said he came up with the plan three years earlier while delivering pizzas to the Yonhi Manor compound.

When he heard that the SFS students took an annual trip to Cheju-do, he convinced the ferry company to allow his speed boat to be used as a special attraction where the SFS classes could purchase items. He knew the students liked to purchase key chains as souvenirs. "Those kids always bought dozens of them!"

He told how he had established a monitoring system to track the movement of each key chain. After a while, he was able to track the movements of various people in the area.

The police captain said it was a very clever idea that had apparently paid off well, since additional members of the robbery ring had been using the same tracking techniques with the families of other businessmen in Seoul.

"Well, one of my wishes really did come true," Claire told Emily and Annie as they walked across the playground during noon recess. "I wished that my family would not be robbed, and it wasn't!"

"Emily, did any of your wishes come true?" asked Annie.

"Yes, actually, more than one came true. You see, I always like it when we do things together. I just kept wishing that we would see another white horse, and then we could make another wish. Now I am waiting for us to see the next white horse!"

The girls laughed and hugged. Then a bell signaled that recess was over, and they walked back inside.

# 15.

# All-School Assembly

The Chief of Police for the city of Seoul was a special guest at the all-school assembly on the first Wednesday of the following month. All the students and teachers from Kindergarten through the twelfth grade sat on chairs in the big gym. Everyone watched in silence as the police chief slowly passed through the aisle from the back of the gym up to the stage. He wore a black uniform and a white captain's hat. Shiny brass buttons on each sleeve matched those on the front of his jacket. His black leather boots hit the floor heavily with each step. His important-looking uniform caused him to appear larger than he really was.

Following a short introduction by the headmaster, the Police Chief greeted the assembly. He spoke softly, which really surprised everyone. His English was easy to understand and he had a warm smile.

"He reminds me of my grandpa," whispered Jack to Craig. The boys glanced at each other and bumped their shoulders as they continued to listen.

"To all of you at Seoul Foreign School, I bring greetings from the Seoul Metropolitan Police Agency as well as the Head Office for the city of Seoul. As you know, the residents in this neighborhood have been victimized by petty robberies for some time. Today I am happy to report that the thieves responsible for these break-ins have been identified. Their punishment will be decided by our court system in the near future."

The police chief continued to speak, encouraging everyone to establish strong values, good work habits, honesty, courage, dependable personalities, and other characteristics of good citizens. Near the end of his talk, he focused directly on the sixth-grade class.

"I am here today to bring special recognition to seven students from the sixth-grade class for their assistance to help solve this case. They demonstrated outstanding citizenship qualities as they worked together with diligence and responsibility to track down clues along the way. They have proven once again that real heroes may not always be adults. Age has nothing to do with it. You can make a difference no matter what age you are."

Then, he asked the seven students to come up on the stage so they could each be given a special certificate. Everyone stood and clapped and cheered as the three girls and four boys walked to the stage. With the students standing beside him, the police chief held up a certificate. "Each of these students will receive a framed certificate like the one in my hand. It is the Outstanding Citizenship Award. The city of Seoul gives these awards to individuals who by their actions have demonstrated outstanding qualities as good citizens. Notice that the certificate carries the signature of the Mayor of Seoul and a gold seal embossed with the imprint of the Korean National Treasure Number One, the Namdaemun Gate.

***Outstanding Citizenship Award***

After the students received their awards, the headmaster thanked the police chief for his visit to SFS. The high school choir led everyone in the song, "Shine Jesus Shine." Then, the school chaplain closed the assembly with a prayer, thanking God for bringing good blessings out of a bad problem.

# 16.

# The Cat's Tale
# and the Bird's Nest

Later that afternoon, Mrs. Van returned home from her weekly trip to the Costco store. As she parked the car by the fence near the F building, she noticed a bright reflection from an object in what appeared to be a small pile of leaves. Stepping out of the car, she kicked at the pile and knelt to get a closer look. The messy collection had the look of an over-turned waste basket, with all sorts of litter thrown together. She found the shiny object and picked it up. It was a whistle on a chain. An identification tag was also attached. "Yonhi Manor Security" was imprinted on the tag. "I wonder how this got here?" she said to herself. She rubbed it clean and put it into her pocket. "I'll take it to the guard house later."

Using a long twig to poke through rest of the pile, she spotted a dirty pink comb with missing teeth, a Barbie doll's head with no hair, a red and black plastic spider, and a tiny broken picture frame. These were all things from her apartment. "This must be Tigger's work," she said aloud. Just then the cat quietly slinked around the corner. Coming closer, Tigger stretched fully and then sat on the grass.

**Tigger stretched fully**

"No more of this!" Mrs. Van said, as she pointed to the pile of trash. "What were you trying to do? Make a nest? Leave that to the birds!"

In the fading sunlight, Yazdee sat wearily on her large warm nest. She cocked her head and listened. From somewhere far away, she heard the evening call of a cuckoo bird. For many days now, she watched for the man with the shiny helmet who rode the fancy motorbike. His *WE DO PIZZA* business in this area seemed to have come to an end.

His secret other business must have been finally discovered. It had taken everyone else a long time to solve the mystery. She knew all about it from the beginning to the end. Yazdee had seen it all take place under her watchful eye!

Tonight the bird was restless. She wiggled and ruffled her wings. She moved awkwardly to stretch each of her stiff legs. Suddenly her eyes opened wide. She jumped up! Something in her nest was moving! Her sudden loud squawk pierced the air! Yazdee's eggs were beginning to hatch!

*Yazdee's eggs were beginning to hatch!*

~The End~

LaVergne, TN USA
26 July 2010
190919LV00002B/2/P